You were always JEALOUS of this lamp

INSIGHTS

an imprint of

INSIGHT EDITIONS

www.insighteditions.com

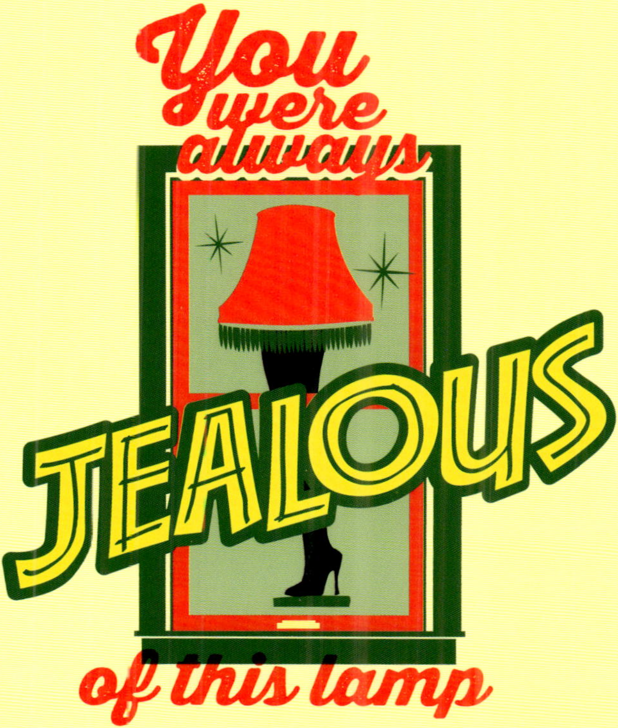
You
were
always
JEALOUS
of this lamp

INSIGHTS

an imprint of

INSIGHT EDITIONS

www.insighteditions.com

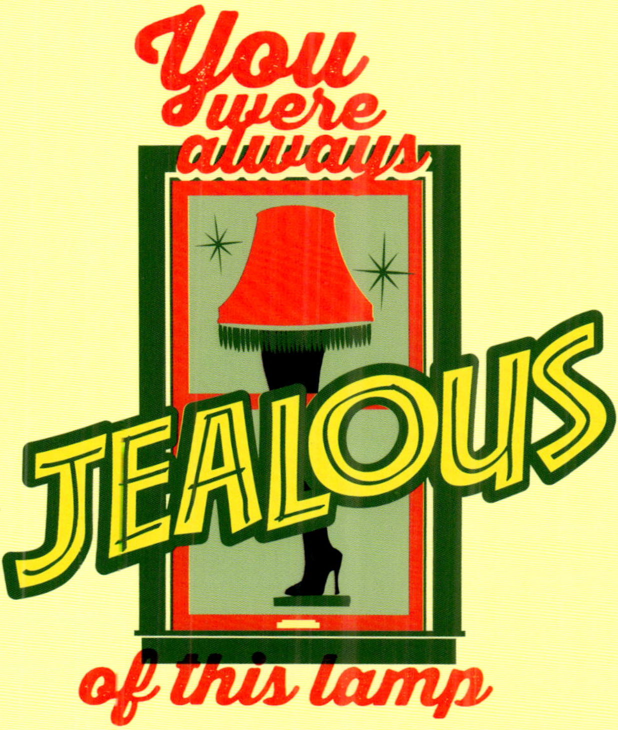
You
were
always
JEALOUS
of this lamp

INSIGHTS

an imprint of

INSIGHT EDITIONS

www.insighteditions.com

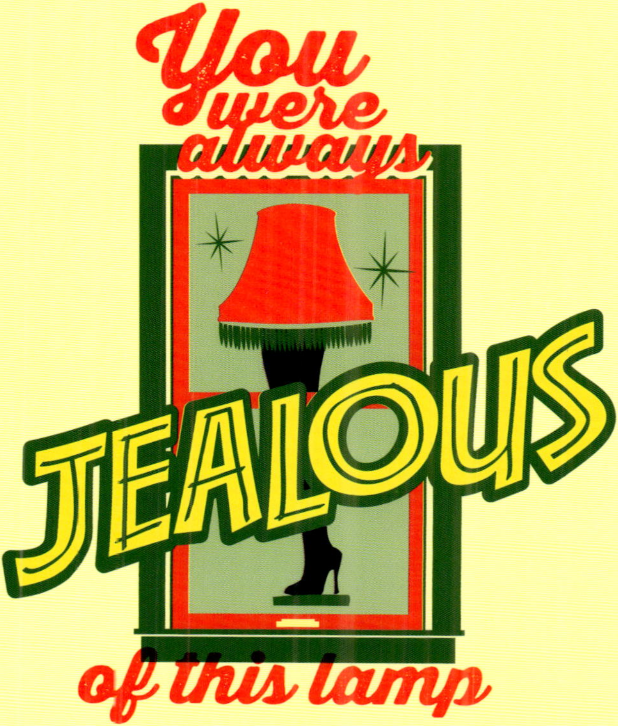
You
were
always
JEALOUS
of this lamp

INSIGHTS

an imprint of

INSIGHT EDITIONS

www.insighteditions.com

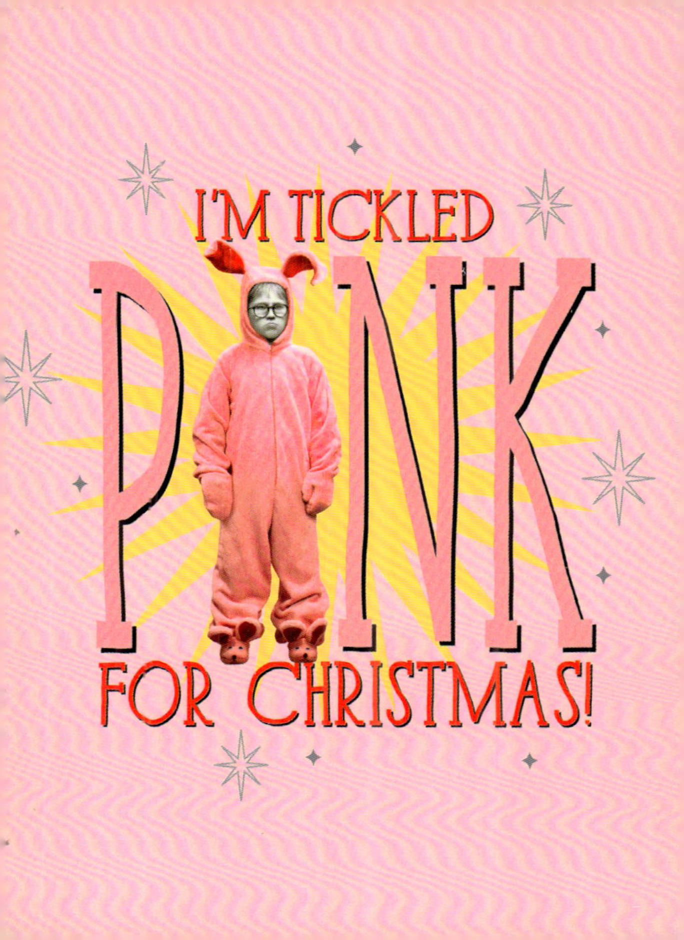
I'M TICKLED
PINK
FOR CHRISTMAS!

INSIGHTS

an imprint of

INSIGHT EDITIONS

www.insighteditions.com

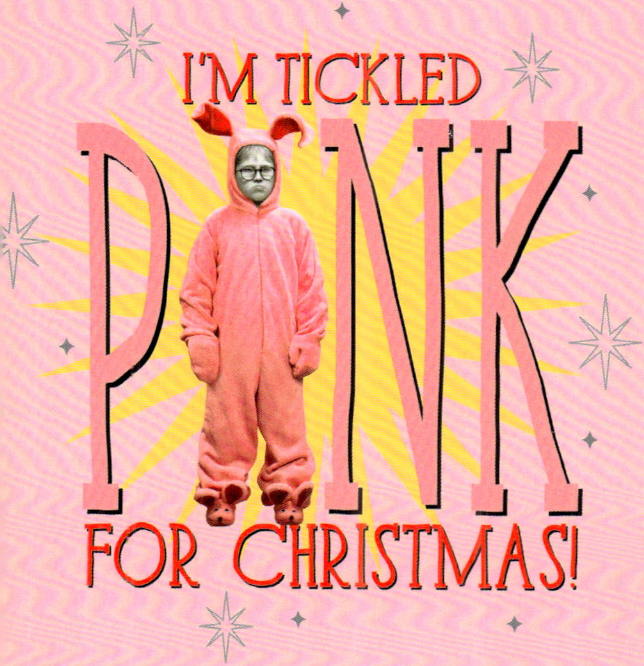
I'M TICKLED
PINK
FOR CHRISTMAS!

INSIGHTS

an imprint of

INSIGHT EDITIONS

www.insighteditions.com

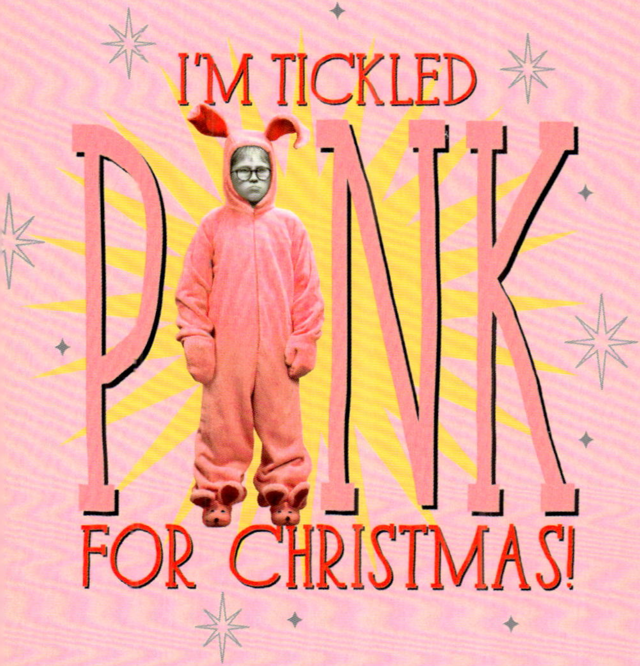
I'M TICKLED
PINK
FOR CHRISTMAS!

INSIGHTS

an imprint of

INSIGHT EDITIONS

www.insighteditions.com

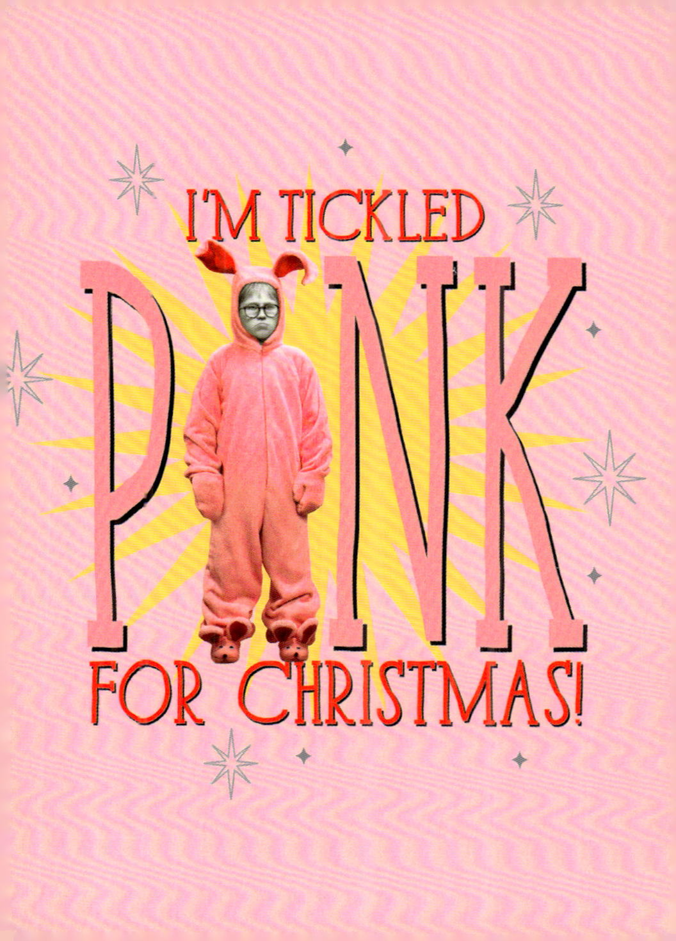
I'M TICKLED
PINK
FOR CHRISTMAS!

INSIGHTS

an imprint of

INSIGHT EDITIONS

www.insighteditions.com

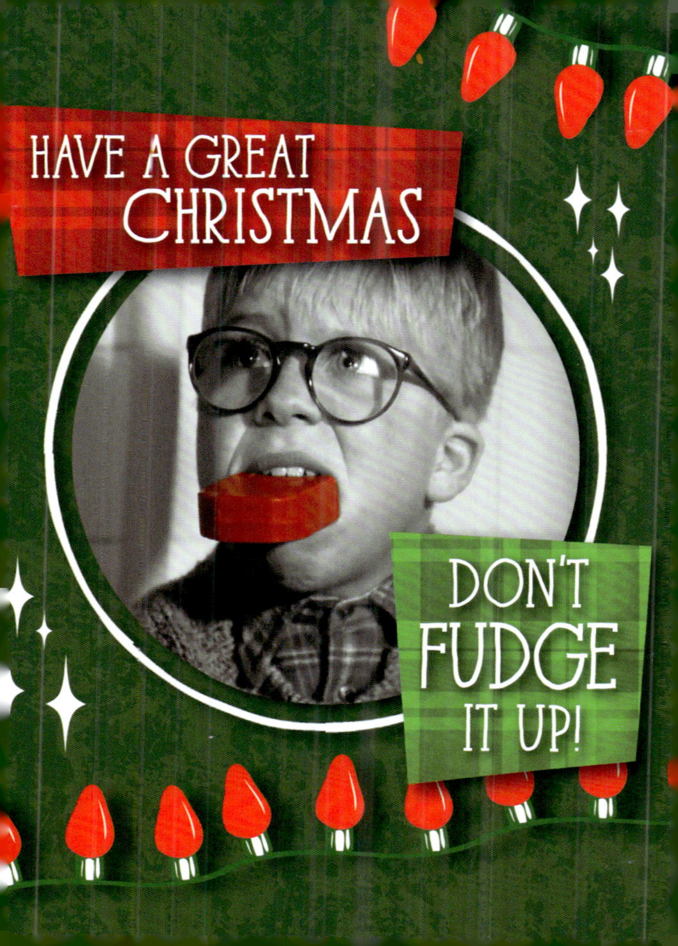
HAVE A GREAT CHRISTMAS
DON'T FUDGE IT UP!

INSIGHTS

an imprint of

INSIGHT EDITIONS

www.insighteditions.com

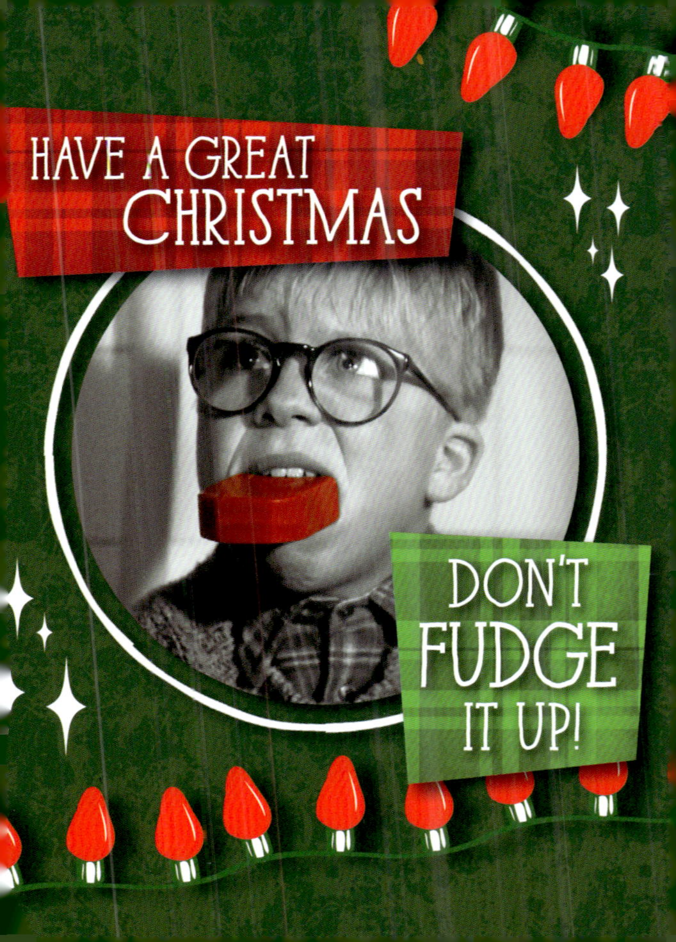
HAVE A GREAT
CHRISTMAS
DON'T
FUDGE
IT UP!

INSIGHTS

an imprint of

INSIGHT EDITIONS

www.insighteditions.com

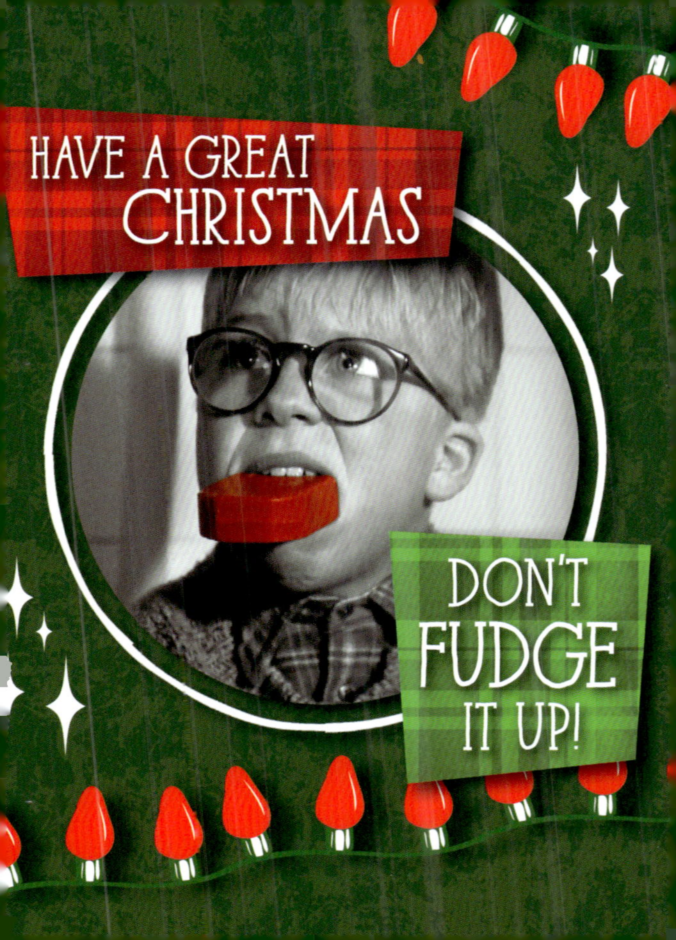
HAVE A GREAT
CHRISTMAS
DON'T
FUDGE
IT UP!

INSIGHTS

an imprint of

INSIGHT EDITIONS

www.insighteditions.com

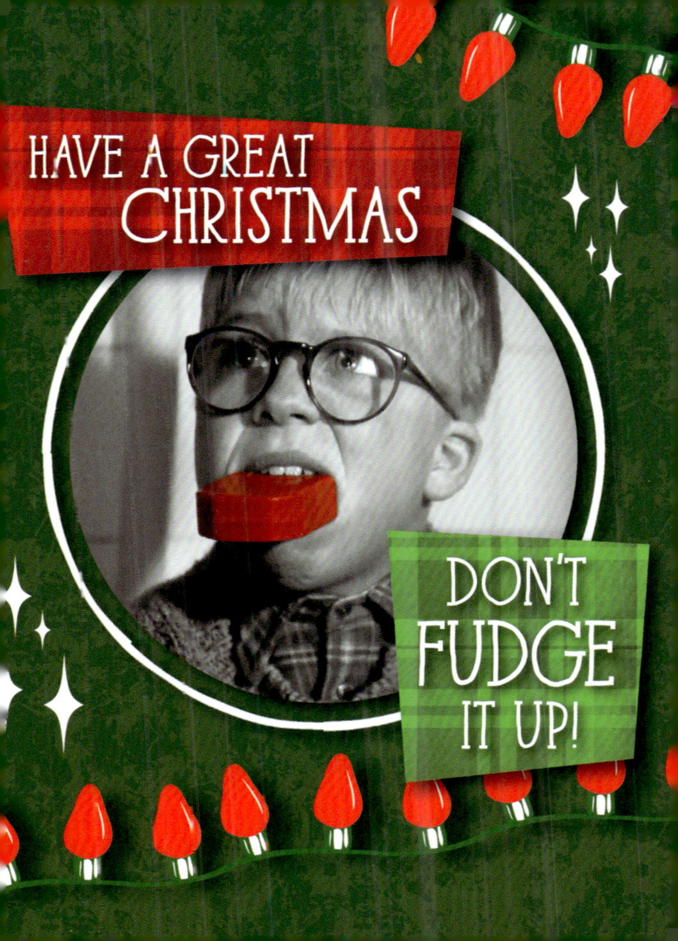
HAVE A GREAT
CHRISTMAS
DON'T
FUDGE
IT UP!

INSIGHTS

an imprint of

INSIGHT EDITIONS

www.insighteditions.com

SEASONS GREETINGS

A Christmas Story

Peace. Harmony. Comfort and Joy...Maybe Next Year.

INSIGHTS
an imprint of
INSIGHT EDITIONS
www.insighteditions.com

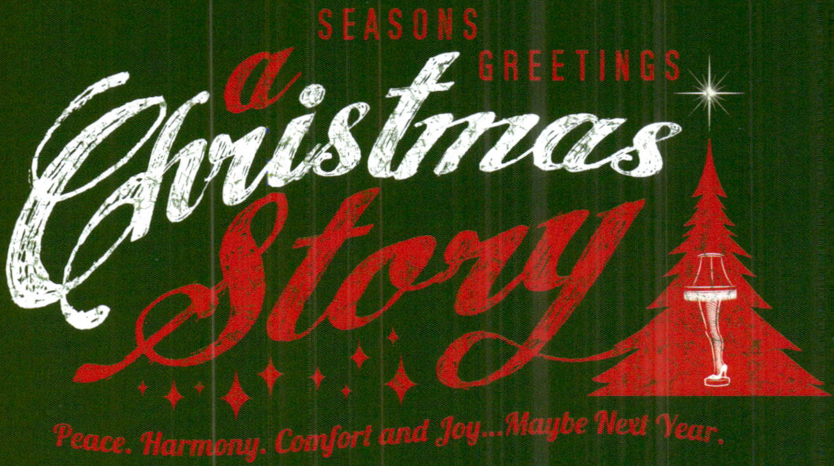
SEASONS GREETINGS
A Christmas Story
Peace. Harmony. Comfort and Joy...Maybe Next Year.

INSIGHTS
an imprint of
INSIGHT EDITIONS
www.insighteditions.com

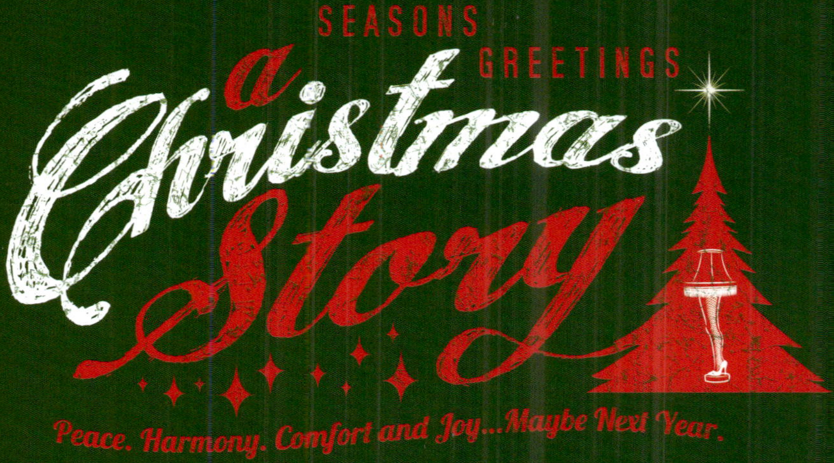
SEASONS GREETINGS
A Christmas Story
Peace. Harmony. Comfort and Joy...Maybe Next Year.

INSIGHTS
an imprint of
INSIGHT EDITIONS
www.insighteditions.com

SEASONS GREETINGS

A Christmas Story

Peace. Harmony. Comfort and Joy...Maybe Next Year.

INSIGHTS
an imprint of
INSIGHT EDITIONS
www.insighteditions.com

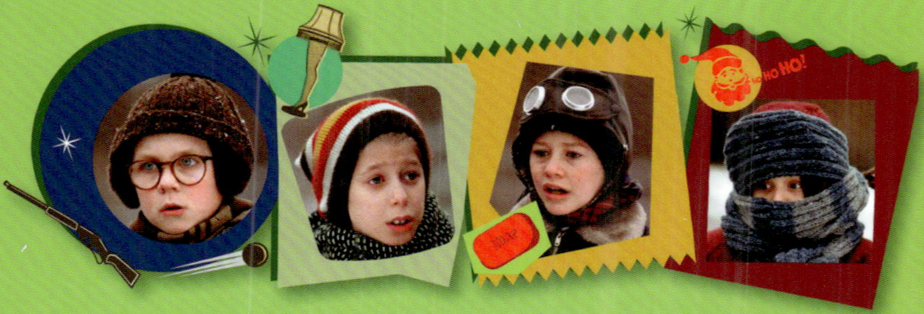

"100% Red-Blooded, Two Fisted, ALL AMERICAN CHRISTMAS"

INSIGHTS
an imprint of
INSIGHT EDITIONS
www.insighteditions.com

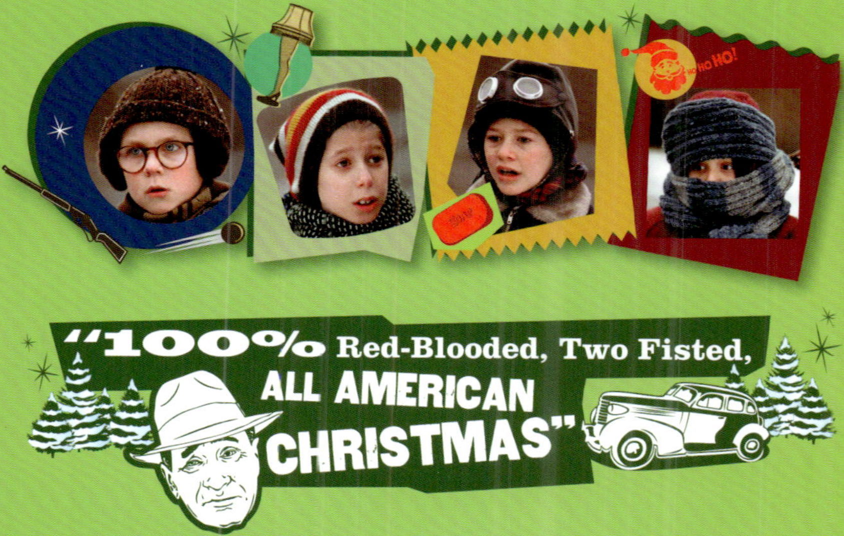
HO HO HO!
“100% Red-Blooded, Two Fisted,
ALL AMERICAN
CHRISTMAS”

INSIGHTS
an imprint of
INSIGHT EDITIONS
www.insighteditions.com

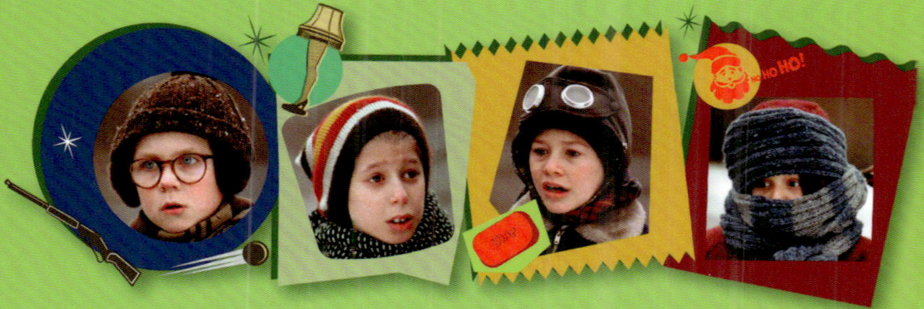

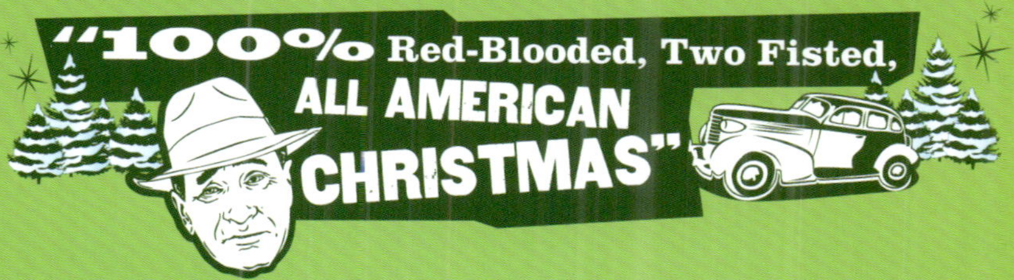
"100% Red-Blooded, Two Fisted,
ALL AMERICAN
CHRISTMAS"

INSIGHTS

an imprint of

INSIGHT EDITIONS

www.insighteditions.com

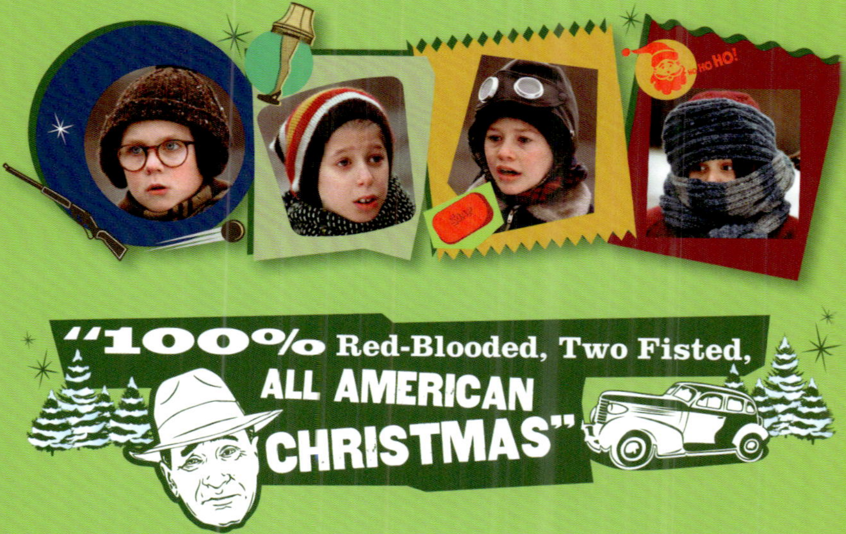
HO HO HO!
"100% Red-Blooded, Two Fisted,
ALL AMERICAN
CHRISTMAS"

INSIGHTS
an imprint of
INSIGHT EDITIONS
www.insighteditions.com